EASY
CHAPTER

DISNEP · PIXAR

WALL·E

A ROBOT'S TALE

A STEPPING STONE BOOK™

Random House New York

Library of Congress Control Number: 2007939446

ISBN: 978-0-7364-2523-0

www.randomhouse.com/kids/disney

Printed in the United States of America

10 9 8 7 6 5 4 3   First Edition

Disney · PIXAR

WALL·E

A ROBOT'S TALE

Adapted by Jillian Joy Samuels
Illustrated by IBOIX estudi

Designed by Stuart Smith of Disney Publishing's Global Design Group
Inspired by the art and designs created by Pixar

CHAPTER 01

▪□□□□□□□□□□□□□□□□□

TIME: The 29th century
PLACE: Earth
ROBOT: A WALL•E unit. (Definition: WALL•E, aka Waste Allocation Load Lifter, Earth class. Pronunciation: WAH-lee, as in English proper name "Wally." Directive: to compact trash into cubes and place those cubes in towers. Goal: to make Earth habitable again for humans who have been temporarily evacuated to outer space.)

Whirrrr. Bzzzzzz! Plunk. WALL•E wandered among the mountainous towers of trash in the hazy air, his treads crunching over layers of garbage. The little dirt-brown, box-shaped robot had a few dents and some replaced parts,

4

but overall he looked okay. Not bad, considering he had spent the past several centuries squishing trash into compacted cubes.

"Dah-dum-dah-dum . . ." The music from WALL•E's recording device echoed between the trash towers WALL•E had built from the trash cubes. He loved this music. It came from his favorite video, *Hello, Dolly!*

Rustle, rustle. WALL•E heard his pet cockroach crawling toward him. The cockroach was WALL•E's only companion.

WALL•E waved to his pet, as if to say, "Time to go home!"

Followed by his cockroach, WALL•E passed an old holo-graphic billboard, still working since the days when people had lived on Earth instead of in outer space. Buy-n-Large, the company that had provided all consumer goods for humans and had practically run the planet, had created this advertisement centuries earlier. They were trying to lure people onto the sleek new spacecraft shown on the ad: "Too much garbage in your face? There's plenty of space out in space! We'll clean up the mess while you're away."

WALL•E hardly listened to the ad anymore. It would probably be a few more centuries before people returned to Earth on that spacecraft. He was, after all, pretty small and the planet was big—and dirty. He had lots more cleaning to do.

At last WALL•E approached an old trailer truck. This was his home.

Inside, he went directly to an old VCR and popped in a battered cassette of *Hello, Dolly!* He hummed along with the music as he placed his newly collected treasures on shelves along with the rest of his items. Then he turned his attention back to the TV. WALL•E studied the movie as it played, watching as two humans lovingly clasped hands. WALL•E locked his own two robotic hands together. He didn't notice anything special. Maybe he needed another robot's hand to clasp, or maybe it was something only humans could do. Still, WALL•E wanted to try it. He wanted to hold hands with another robot and fall in love.

After the movie, WALL•E went outside. *Whoooooosh!* The wind was picking up!

A warning light went off on WALL•E's chest. That meant one thing—a killer dust storm was approaching. WALL•E was used to these. Unfazed, he turned around, went back into the trailer, and closed the door.

Suddenly, WALL•E stopped. He had forgotten the cockroach! WALL•E opened the door and whistled. The cockroach hopped inside and WALL•E closed the door again. As the wind howled outside, WALL•E and the cockroach settled down for the night, the trailer rocking in the storm.

First thing in the morning, WALL•E's charge meter started flashing, cautioning that he was low on power.

"*Uuuuuu*," WALL•E groaned. Slowly, he made his way to the truck's roof and groggily soaked up the sunlight. Finally, he was fully recharged. WALL•E was feeling better and was ready for more trash cubing!

Gathering his work things (and the cock-roach), WALL•E set out for the day. Soon he found a good area to clean and started cubing trash. He also picked up items and examined them, trying them out. He sorted these items into two categories: "Keep" and "Don't Keep."

Paddle ball—That seemed fun . . . until the ball bounced out of control, missed the paddle, and bonked WALL•E on the head repeatedly. (Don't Keep.)

Diamond ring in black box—Interesting. Toss the shiny thing. (Don't Keep.) Hang on to the black box. (Keep.)

Fire extinguisher—Not sure what this was, WALL•E pressed a lever. The fire extinguisher exploded with foam, taking WALL•E for a wild ride. (Don't Keep.)

Then WALL•E turned his attention to a small green thing. He had never seen anything like it. It was soft and delicate and seemed kind of . . . alive. Very carefully, keeping the dirt around the base of its stalky part, WALL•E moved it into an old boot. He would keep this mysterious object for his collection.

At the end of the day, WALL•E headed home. Just outside his trailer, he saw a red dot. He leaned in for a closer look. The dot moved! He chased it. This was fun! And odd. What was it? It jumped all over the place. WALL•E tried to catch the red dot, but it kept bouncing away from his grasp.

What WALL•E did not see was that dozens of other dots were collecting on the ground all around him. They were laser beams!

CHAPTER 02

Three enormous columns of fire instantly surrounded WALL•E. The heat was blistering! *Breeeeep!* He dug a hole in the ground and buried himself.

The fire came from the rockets of a giant spaceship. It hovered above him.

Even though he was terrified, WALL•E still popped his head aboveground. He hadn't seen a working spaceship in centuries! The ship dropped a capsule to the ground, where it unfolded, revealing . . . the single most beautiful creature WALL•E had ever seen! (Of course, he had been living alone with a

cockroach for several centuries.)

She was a robot. White. Egg-shaped. She had captivating blue eye-slits. WALL•E did not know this, but she was a probe-bot—an EVE (Extraterrestrial Vegetation Evaluator).

As the spaceship took off, the new robot flew into the air, making graceful arcs. "OOOoooo!" cried WALL•E. Maybe *she* was his true love, just like in the romantic video! WALL•E was staring dreamily from his hiding place behind a boulder . . . when he accidentally dislodged a few pebbles.

KA-BLAM! The boulder exploded, shot to smithereens. WALL•E's new love apparently had a powerful blaster arm. That was scary! Still, WALL•E followed her, keeping a safe distance just in case. She seemed to be scanning objects, but none of the objects satisfied her. Maybe if WALL•E knew what she was looking for, he could help.

KA-BLAM! She blasted the cockroach!

Luckily, the bug crawled unharmed out of the smoking crater. She allowed the cockroach to creep up her arm. It tickled her. She giggled! WALL•E sighed happily. This meant that she had feelings and that his cockroach amused her. Maybe now he could move closer to her!

But just then, EVE turned and glared directly at WALL•E. The little robot did what he always did when he felt he was in danger: he tucked in his head and limbs, boxing himself into a small, protected cube.

EVE scanned him. *Buzzz!* The results came up negative. Apparently that was good, because EVE didn't even try to shoot him. She tucked her blaster arm close to her side and left.

WALL•E tried very hard not to be noticed as he followed EVE. But it was difficult. When EVE entered an old BnL store, WALL•E attempted to sneak behind a group of old shopping carts. However, he accidentally launched the carts down a flight of stairs. The carts only stopped when they crashed into the front doors of the store—with WALL•E squished in between!

Even if EVE didn't pay much attention to WALL•E, he was fascinated by her. Once, he even secretly took her measurements while she slept. Then he built a sculpture of her out of trash! EVE stared at it for a few moments and then moved on, but WALL•E didn't mind.

He was completely in love—with a trigger-happy, sleek new robot who had absolutely no interest in him. He was not part of her directive.

CHAPTER 03

EVE's directive was to find vegetation, which would prove to humans that Earth could be repopulated. If plants were once again growing on Earth, then people could return home. This was why EVE scanned object after object. But none showed any sign of life.

Finally, EVE came across an old ship. When again she found no plant life, her frustration finally overflowed. She blasted the ship to bits. WALL·E looked at her sympathetically as she slumped against an anchor.

She looked sad. Cautiously, he approached.

"HumMMMmm." EVE made an odd noise.

WALL·E had no clue as to what she was saying. But the very fact that she was addressing him caused him to topple over backward in shock.

"BZZZwaaa-ooo?" EVE was making more noises. She was communicating! But WALL·E didn't understand any of it, so he couldn't answer. He wished he had found some instructions about communicating in his trash piles.

At last, EVE asked, "Directive?"

"OoooHHH!" WALL·E was thrilled because he finally understood what she meant. She wanted to know what his directive was.

Quickly, he loaded a pile of trash into his compactor and popped out a cube.

Then WALL·E struggled to say the word back to EVE: "Diii . . . rec . . . t—"

"Directive!" EVE shouted. She understood him!

WALL·E nodded enthusiastically. Yes! What was *her* directive?

"Classified," EVE replied.

"Oh." WALL•E was disappointed. Now what could they talk about?

"Szzzzzooooowaaazooorrrrnnn-ame?" EVE asked.

WALL•E took a guess at what she was asking and answered, "WALL•E!"

"Wwwaaaa-lllleeeee," EVE repeated. Apparently, WALL•E had guessed right and they were introducing themselves.

When EVE told WALL•E her name, WALL•E repeated, "Eee-vah." His pronunciation wasn't quite right, but after several more tries, both robots seemed to agree that it was good enough for now.

Just then, WALL•E noticed another killer dust storm coming up fast. Soon dirt, sand, and trash blew all around, nearly smothering them.

CHAPTER 04

WALL·E led EVE through the storm and brought her home to his trailer. It had been a close call, but WALL·E still felt very happy. EVE was here, and he couldn't wait to hold her hand, just like on the video!

"Breeeeep!" EVE raised her blaster arm at something on the wall. She was aiming at a singing fish toy WALL·E had hung up. (WALL·E made a quick note to himself: When attempting to hold hands, be careful of blaster arm.)

WALL·E calmed EVE and led her farther into his truck. Aside from that blaster arm,

WALL•E loved everything about EVE. He wanted to show her all his things. And he had a lot of things to show.

"EEEeeeeee!" WALL•E screamed suddenly. EVE was unraveling his *Hello, Dolly!* video! Quickly, he grabbed the tape back and rewound it. He stuck it into the VCR. Whew! It still worked! Now he could show her how to dance and hold hands. WALL•E grabbed an old hubcap and used it like a hat, dancing around EVE.

Soon EVE began to dance, too. Actually, she spun—at about a thousand miles an hour! Yikes! EVE accidentally hit WALL•E at super-speed, knocking one of his eyes clear across the room.

EVE stopped and made a sad sound. *"Oooorrzz."* She looked so concerned and sorry that WALL•E's heart almost broke. He waved to calm her down, then quickly showed her that he had spare parts: one new eye sensor coming up! Into WALL•E's eye socket it went. WALL•E was used to performing self-repair. It was particularly nice when the replacement parts worked. Now he could see again.

Then WALL•E thought of something perfect. He would show EVE the soft green thing he had found earlier. He didn't know it was a plant. He didn't know that EVE's directive was to find signs of life—to find vegetation. He didn't know that once she saw the plant, she would snatch it with her tractor beam and pull it away, enclosing it in her chest cavity. He also didn't know that this single action would cause her to shut down, leaving only a green light flashing on her chest plate.

CHAPTER 05

WALL•E could not awaken EVE. He didn't understand what had happened. One minute he was showing her the green thing, and the next she was sleeping. He had to do something! He loved her!

WALL•E took EVE to the roof of his trailer, where he recharged with solar energy every morning. But the sun did not wake EVE.

Even though she didn't move, WALL•E took her everywhere. He kept her safe. He held an umbrella over her during a thunderstorm and got struck by lightning. He held another umbrella over her and got struck by lightning again. "Owww!" he cried. Love hurt. Lovers should avoid thunderstorms.

WALL•E kept going, but EVE slept on. Eventually, WALL•E started cubing trash again, but his heart wasn't in it. Now that he knew what true love was, he wanted it back. He liked love.

One day, WALL•E was cubing trash when he saw a large bright glow above his trailer. It was right where he had left EVE! WALL•E sped up his treads and raced toward home.

It was the spaceship that had dropped EVE on Earth. Now it had returned to pick her up!

"Eeeee!" WALL•E exclaimed, whipping his treads across Earth's surface. *"Eee-vah! Eee-vah!"* The ship's robotic arms lifted EVE from the roof of WALL•E's trailer, drawing her inside. Then its rocket engines powered up in a fiery blaze. WALL•E kept racing toward the ship that now held EVE.

WALL•E quickly glanced behind him and saw his cockroach.

Beep! WALL•E ordered the cockroach to stay. WALL•E's pet sat down sadly. WALL•E didn't want him coming along. This could be dangerous.

With no time to spare, WALL•E latched on to the side of the ship. WALL•E knew he had to be brave for EVE. He tightened his grip on a metal support beam and screamed as the ship blasted into space.

After a while, the spacecraft exited Earth's atmosphere, and WALL•E relaxed as the powerful force of gravity lessened.

"Oooooh!" he said as he glanced back at Earth. It looked really cool from up there. Whoops! WALL•E quickly realized that the pull of gravity had been replaced by a sensation of floating. It was time to hold on tight again. He looked below him and saw a window. EVE was inside the ship!

"Eee-vah!" WALL•E shouted, knocking on the window. But she didn't respond. She was still sleeping. Or maybe she was permanently damaged. This worried WALL•E, and he thought long and hard about it. If EVE was broken, he would fix her. He would help her, and he would stay with her. That was what the people in the movie did when they were in love. He might be a robot, but he knew an awful lot about love. After all, he must have seen *Hello, Dolly!* approximately 519,462 times.

Of course, before WALL•E could fix EVE, he had to figure out a way to get to her. This could be hard. She was locked inside the ship. He was locked outside. WALL•E wondered if the ship had plans to stop somewhere during the next century.

Just as he was pondering this notion, he saw that the ship seemed to be heading toward an odd-shaped planet. But it wasn't a planet. It was another ship . . . a gigantic ship! And the little spacecraft he was riding was headed right into a tiny hole on its side: the docking bay.

CHAPTER 06

This gigantic ship was the *Axiom*, a massive star liner carrying thousands of human passengers. The passengers were enjoying themselves in space, but they were also waiting for the time when Earth would be clean again and they could return home. By now, however, these passengers had been waiting a long time. In fact, all of them had been born on the *Axiom*. Even their great-great-grandparents had been born on the *Axiom*! No one, not even the Captain, had any real idea what Earth looked like anymore.

With so many people on board, there were lots of robots, too. WALL·E had not seen

another robot (except EVE) for centuries. So he felt a little surprised to see so many in the docking bay. One working bot lifted EVE out of the spaceship. Another scrubbed her. Others raced around the docking bay, performing all kinds of functions.

WALL•E chased after EVE, trying to stay hidden—especially from the cleaning-bots. (It might take them a year to scrub WALL•E clean!) Their leader was named M-O—he was a microbe obliterator. Suddenly, M-O seemed to pick up on WALL•E's dirty presence. His scanner read 100% FOREIGN CONTAMINANT.

A flashing red light and siren popped out of M-O's head as he charged toward WALL•E.

But WALL•E wanted to stay with EVE. She was being carted off! Not knowing what else to do, WALL•E wiped one of his filthy treads on M-O's face. As M-O recoiled in disgust and maniacally began cleaning himself, WALL•E sped away.

"Eee-vah!" he shouted. He raced over and jumped onto the back of the transport that was taking her away.

Holding on as tightly as he could, WALL•E watched as Gopher, the Captain's tiny valet-bot, drove them to the lowest deck of the huge ship. They were in the *Axiom*'s service corridor. It was filled with robots—all the latest models, all new and shiny.

Whoosh! While WALL•E glanced around in wonder, EVE's transport zipped away from him. He zigzagged his way in and out of the traffic, occasionally bumping into other robots of all shapes and sizes.

At last, WALL•E spotted the transport going up a ramp. He made it out of a robot traffic jam and continued to follow EVE.

As he arrived at the economy-class level of the ship, WALL•E saw the first humans he had seen in a very long time. These people seemed different from the ones he remembered. Not one of them was walking. They all sat in hover chairs, staring at monitors. They seemed to have forgotten how to walk around and do things for themselves.

"Happy *Axiom* Day!" a voice said over a loudspeaker.

Crash! Whoa! A passenger knocked into WALL•E and fell off his hover chair. All the hover chairs behind came to a stop while the human lay on the ground. But the human didn't try to stand or even sit. He didn't seem to know what to do. Neither did WALL•E.

"A service-bot will be here to assist you momentarily," a steward-bot told the human. "Please remain stationary."

WALL•E was relieved. He wanted to help, but he really needed to save EVE. Where was she? Just in the nick of time, WALL•E spotted EVE being lifted onto a monorail. He motored over at top speed and jumped onto the last car.

"Attention, *Axiom* shoppers! Try blue—it's the new red!" an announcement blared over a loudspeaker. Almost immediately, everyone's jumpsuits turned from red to blue.

WALL•E sneaked behind a passenger named Mary as he tried to move toward the front of the monorail. But Mary was talking on her video monitor and wasn't paying attention to anything around her. And there wasn't enough room for WALL•E to squeeze past. He was stuck.

WALL·E politely waved his arms behind Mary's holo-screen. She didn't notice. Finally, he yanked on her speaker headrest, trying to pull himself up to get her attention.

Instantly, Mary's holo-screen shorted out. Stunned, she looked around. She didn't know what to do without her holo-screen. She looked at her feet. She wiggled her toes. And then . . . she shifted forward in her hover chair to get a better view of the ship. Little did WALL·E know that he was changing the course of history. Because of him, someone on the *Axiom* was acting on her own, even showing curiosity. This was a first.

But WALL•E had no time to observe. He raced toward EVE.

He caught up just in time to ride with her to the Captain's bridge. WALL•E was careful to stay hidden, but he was thrilled to be near EVE again. As they entered the bridge, the Captain's wheel disengaged from the front control panel and moved toward them, sliding on tracks connected to the ceiling.

Called Auto (aka Autopilot), the wheel was a bot with a single camera eye in the center of his circular body. A periscope stem connected him to the ceiling. WALL•E noticed that Auto scanned EVE up and down, taking particular interest in the green light glowing on her chest plate.

And then, without warning, WALL•E dropped through a hole in the floor.

CHAPTER 07

WALL·E landed in the Captain's personal quarters, just below the bridge. There the little bot quickly boxed himself to try to remain unseen. Luckily, a crowd of prep-bots swarmed into the room to awaken the Captain and prepare him for his day. They combed, shaved, and even dressed the Captain. Trying to blend in, WALL·E pretended to be a foot-bot. It was not his best idea. Wiggling the Captain's toes, WALL·E made the human giggle.

Finally, the Captain's chair rose to the bridge, with WALL·E clinging to the bottom.

There she was—EVE—on the bridge, still

beautiful in her sleep.

Auto reported all the ship's daily updates to the Captain. As usual, they were the same as every previous day, except . . . the Captain noticed a flashing button on the console.

"Auto, what is—" the Captain began.

As if responding to the Captain's question, Auto turned to EVE.

Looking over, the Captain saw that she had a flashing light on her chest, too. It matched the light on the console.

"Eee-vah!" WALL•E sighed, watching with joy as Auto turned EVE on. She was alive! The Captain pushed EVE's flashing green light and EVE lit up, projecting a holo-graphic video across the room.

"Greetings and congratulations, Captain!" The holo-screen came to life with a prerecorded message from the BnL CEO. "If you're seeing this, that means your Extraterrestrial Vegetation Evaluator—or 'EVE' probe—has returned from Earth with a confirmed specimen of ongoing photosynthesis. That's right—it means it's time to go back home!"

"Home!" exclaimed the Captain. "Does he mean *home* home?"

Auto nodded. The holo-screen message continued: "Now that Earth has been restored to a life-sustaining status, by golly, we can begin *Operation: Recolonize*!"

WALL•E thought about this. EVE had needed to come to this ship to deliver the green thing so that all the passengers could go back to Earth. That meant that WALL•E and EVE could go back to Earth, too, and live happily ever after, dancing and singing—just like in the romantic video!

While the Captain was busy trying to read the *Operation: Recolonize* manual, WALL•E sidled up to EVE and cheerfully tapped on her shoulder.

"WALL•E?" EVE looked shocked, almost angry to see him.

"Eee-vah . . . ," WALL•E said, confused by her behavior.

EVE shoved WALL•E behind her to hide him. The Captain was approaching.

"Well, let's open her up," the Captain said.

EVE's chest cavity was opened up. But the plant was gone!

CHAPTER 08

As Auto and the Captain turned around to reread the manual, EVE remained frozen, stunned.

"Eee-vah?" WALL•E asked, still hiding from the others. He wanted to help EVE.

"Plant!" EVE snapped in reply. She thought WALL•E had stolen the plant!

The Captain sighed. "The probe must be defective," he said. "Send her to the repair ward." As commanded, Gopher put EVE in a freeze ray, lifting her off the floor . . . and revealing WALL•E.

WALL•E felt all eyes on him. There was

dead silence in the room.

"And fix that robot as well," the Captain said, pointing at WALL•E. "Have it hosed down or something. It's filthy."

Phew! Well, at least now WALL•E didn't have to hide. And maybe he could help EVE find the plant. As they headed off on the transport, WALL•E knew that EVE was still angry with him. He wondered how he could get her to realize that he hadn't taken the plant.

Soon they reached the repair ward. EVE was taken to a back room for special repairs, while WALL•E tried to evade the ward's orderlies. Then a defective beautician-bot painted WALL•E's face with hideous colors. Finally, he was locked up next to a group of malfunctioning bots. A paint-bot rapidly flung his paintbrush back and forth, causing paint to fly everywhere. A vacuum-bot sneezed dust in WALL•E's face.

But WALL•E hardly noticed. He was

completely focused on EVE, and when he saw her blaster arm being detached in the diagnostics room, he thought she was being tortured. Panicked, WALL•E cried out, "Eee-vah!"

Activating the laser beam between his eyes, WALL•E cut himself free from his restraints and smashed his way into the diagnostics room. Grabbing EVE's blaster arm, he swung it backward . . . and accidentally triggered it. *KA-BLAM!* The repair ward control panel exploded.

Uh-oh, thought WALL•E. He hadn't meant to break such a big, important thing.

"WALL•E!" EVE screamed.

With the control panel destroyed, all the energy bands that held the robots captive dissolved and the repair ward's door slid open. The reject-bots were free! In that brief moment, little WALL•E became a hero—well, at least to the reject-bots. They carried him out on their shoulders, cheering loudly.

Unfortunately, the celebration didn't last.

"Halt!" called a steward-bot.

As the group stopped, EVE flew in and grabbed her blaster arm away from WALL•E. But as she reattached the arm, a steward snapped their picture. It looked like she was using her blaster arm as a weapon! She and WALL•E seemed like dangerous criminals.

"Caution: rogue robots! Caution: rogue robots!" Loudspeakers broadcast warnings all over the ship. Now WALL•E, EVE, and the rest of the reject-bots were really in trouble. Passengers panicked.

At last, EVE grabbed WALL•E and flew him high above the commotion. Then, as EVE glanced out a window, she hesitated. She had an idea.

CHAPTER 09

It took some effort to evade all the steward-bots, but soon, WALL•E and EVE were inside the life-pod bay. EVE hovered at the console, pushing buttons. WALL•E peeked at her hand and then privately interlocked his own hands—just as he had done back home, when he watched the romantic video. Maybe, just maybe . . . He could almost reach out and hold her hand right now.

"Eee-vah . . . ?" WALL•E whispered. He would finally ask her to hold his hand.

FLASH! The long, dark room grew bright. There before them was a tiny ship—a life pod.

EVE led WALL•E to it and gestured for him to go inside. WALL•E gleamed with excitement. Plopping down on the seat, he patted the place next to him, inviting EVE to join him. He thought that this was their chance to escape. They could fly away together, alone. The perfect time for him to hold her hand!

"WALL•E," EVE said, turning to leave. She wanted to send him safely back to Earth while she stayed behind on the *Axiom* to complete her directive.

Nooooo! WALL•E thought. He ran out of the pod toward EVE. He would not leave without her!

Just then, the elevator chimed. Someone was coming. EVE and WALL•E hid in a dark corner. Gopher entered the room and approached the pod, dropping something inside: the plant!

The plant was still alive, on the ship. And Gopher had had it all along!

When Gopher turned to the control panel, WALL•E joyfully raced into the life pod to retrieve the plant. Now EVE will be really happy, WALL•E thought. Finding that plant was her directive. Now she could rest . . . and be with WALL•E!

"WALL•E!" EVE shouted in warning.

It was too late. Gopher punched some buttons on the console, then pushed the launch button. WALL•E was trapped inside the life pod. He was blasted into space!

"Eeeeeeee!" WALL•E screamed as the life pod hurtled into space. Frantically, he pushed all the buttons on the life pod's console. Finally, the electronic voice on the console responded: "Pod will self-destruct in ten seconds."

Ohhhh, no! WALL•E thought. Panicking, he looked around the pod and saw a fire extinguisher. He recognized it from that time on Earth. WALL•E quickly opened the escape hatch and turned on the fire extinguisher.

KA-BOOM! The life pod exploded and WALL•E was tossed into space. He used the fire extinguisher to propel himself away from the explosion. Zooming through space was fun! When EVE flew out to rescue him, WALL•E zipped right past her. Wheee!

It took a few moments for EVE to catch up with WALL•E. When she did, WALL•E opened up his chest and EVE could see that he still had the plant.

"WALL•E!" EVE shrieked with delight. Quickly, she tucked the plant into her chest. Then she pulled WALL•E close, spinning him

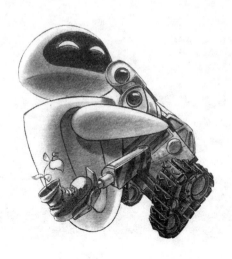

around happily. Suddenly, a tiny arc of electricity passed between their heads. It was a robot kiss.

"OOooo!" WALL·E exclaimed. His energy meter began to glow.

WALL·E was thrilled. As the two robots started back toward the *Axiom,* he pressed the lever on his fire extinguisher and gleefully zoomed ahead. EVE followed. Together they swooped around the ship.

Meanwhile, inside the *Axiom*, Mary looked out the window and saw WALL•E and EVE dancing in space. Surprised, she pulled over another passenger, John, to watch with her. Mary turned John's holo-screen off, just as WALL•E had turned hers off earlier. John and Mary both began to look around and notice things other than their holo-screens.

Seconds later, WALL•E and EVE flew past the Captain's window. The Captain was busy looking up information about Earth in the ship's computer. Oddly, WALL•E seemed to be awakening passengers on the ship, making them more interested in the world around them.

When his fire extinguisher sputtered, empty at last, WALL•E saw EVE fly toward him. Crooning happily, he let her carry him to an open portal at the side of the ship.

CHAPTER 10

Back inside the *Axiom*, EVE quickly led WALL·E toward the lido deck, making sure they weren't seen by anyone. They were still considered rogue robots, armed and dangerous. WALL·E had never imagined that he would be thought of as dangerous. Then again, he had never dreamed he might find someone like EVE. And now here he was, in love!

But once they got near the bridge lobby, they saw a line of steward-bots on guard. How could EVE and WALL·E get around them? How could they get up to the Captain?

EVE and WALL·E hid near the pool and

tried to figure out a plan. At least, EVE tried to figure out a plan. WALL•E started to think about how nice it would be to hold EVE's hand. He gestured to her, holding out his own hands, then interlocking them. See? It would be so easy to do!

But EVE shook her head. She still didn't understand. WALL•E felt sad.

EVE's gaze returned to the steward-bots. She needed to finish her directive. She had to deliver the plant to the Captain and place it in the holo-detector. Watching her, WALL•E realized how important that mission was for EVE.

Well then, WALL•E thought, he would just have to help. Besides, once EVE accomplished her directive, the *Axiom* would return to Earth. Then EVE and WALL•E could live there together. Earth was better than the *Axiom* anyway—much less confusing, and with lots of neat things to find in the trash.

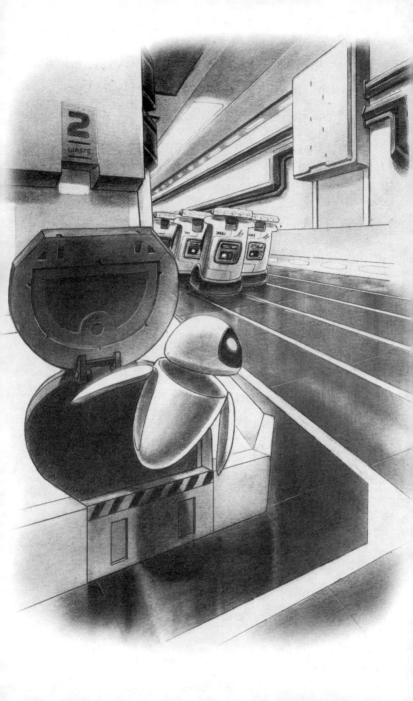

EVE had an idea. She would fly up the trash chute to the Captain's bridge. If she flew very fast, the steward-bots might not see her go by.

But WALL•E wanted to go with her. He could help her! He was an expert on trash, including trash chutes . . . maybe. She might need him.

But EVE gestured to him to stay. WALL•E felt disappointed. Still, maybe things weren't all bad. Maybe EVE cared for him and wanted to keep him safe. WALL•E rocked on his treads and nearly tipped over. He was a googly-eyed robot in love.

He waved to his girlfriend as she zoomed through the bridge lobby. She flew so fast that the steward-bots didn't even notice her. Quickly, she found the entrance to the trash chute and opened the lid. A moment later, she was gone, zipping up the trash chute, straight to the bridge.

CHAPTER 11

While WALL·E waited patiently (well, not really patiently—but at least he waited . . . for a bit), a lot of important things happened. At first, the Captain was thrilled when EVE delivered the plant to him. Happily, he activated the holo-graphic recordings of EVE's time spent on Earth. He wanted to know what Earth looked like. The pictures, however, were strange and brown. As he watched, the Captain became very worried about the bad shape the planet was in.

But soon (and more important for WALL·E), up popped images from WALL·E's *Hello,*

Dolly! video. The sight of people dancing and singing made the Captain feel much happier and more hopeful.

Then (and most important for WALL•E) EVE noticed something else on the video: She saw a human couple holding hands. EVE finally understood what WALL•E had been trying to do. He had wanted to hold *her* hand! And when the images of her in sleep mode appeared onscreen, she saw how WALL•E had taken such good, loving care of her.

"WALL•E," she said tenderly.

Of course, WALL•E didn't see or hear this. He was still waiting on the deck below, hiding behind a towel cart next to the pool. Softly, he chanted, "Eee-vah! Eee-vah!" He was practicing how he would offer his hand to EVE and finally get her to hold it. After all, soon she would finish her directive. Then she would be ready for other things, like holding hands!

The more WALL•E thought about it, the

more excited he became. Finally, he couldn't wait any longer. He had to find EVE right away!

WALL•E boxed himself and pushed the towel cart along, careful to stay behind it. Slowly, he crept past the passengers who sat by the pool. Carefully, he moved past the line of steward-bots still on guard in the lobby.

At last he reached the trash chute. "Eee-vahhh!" he shouted into it. He heard a loud echo, but no answer. There was only one thing to do. WALL•E crawled into the chute and began to climb up to EVE.

And this time, EVE really did need help.

CHAPTER 12

"Auto, look!" The Captain proudly held up the plant as the robotic autopilot moved down from the ceiling. "We're going home. We can activate the holo-detector!"

"Sir, we cannot go home," Auto announced.

The Captain was shocked. "What are you talking about? Why not?"

At first, Auto would not explain, saying it was classified information. "Tell me what's classified!" the Captain insisted. "That's an order!"

"Aye-aye, sir," Auto finally replied.

Then Auto showed the Captain a top-secret video message from the BnL chairman, sent

from Earth long ago. It was addressed to all the autopilots on star liners carrying passengers who were waiting to return to Earth.

"Hey there, autopilots!" the BnL chairman said. "Uh, got some bad news. *Operation: Cleanup* has, uh, well . . . failed." The chairman was wearing an oxygen mask. "Rising toxicity levels have made life unsustainable on Earth." He told the autopilots to keep all the ships in deep space and not to return to Earth. Ever. "It would be best," he added, "if the Captain and passengers didn't know about this at all."

The video turned itself off. Everyone was silent.

Then Auto asked for the plant.

But the Captain refused. He was thinking really, really hard for the first time in a really, really long time—maybe for the first time ever. "This doesn't make sense," he said. "If Probe One came back with the plant, then life on Earth *is* sustainable! We *can* go back!"

Auto did not argue. Instead, he summoned Gopher, who snatched the plant from the Captain, using a suspension beam. It was becoming clear that Gopher was working for Auto, and that Auto's directive was to get rid of the plant!

"This is mutiny!" the Captain shouted. Then he turned to EVE. "Probe One, arrest Auto."

Obediently, EVE raised her blaster arm. Auto retreated.

"Probe One, you are to put this plant straight into the holo-detector. That's an order!" the Captain shouted.

EVE nodded and shifted her aim toward Gopher. Using his suspension beam, Gopher moved the plant toward EVE, as if to give it to her. Suddenly, he stopped . . . and tossed the plant into the trash chute!

The Captain gasped. Had Auto won?

That was when WALL•E popped out of the trash chute. And he had the plant on his head!

He had caught it while climbing up to the bridge. He looked at EVE happily because he knew she would be glad.

ZZZAPP! Suddenly, Auto poked a prod at WALL•E's chest, causing electric arcs to zoom all around and through him. WALL•E collapsed, burned and still.

EVE watched in horror, but there was nothing she could do. Gopher had caught her in a freeze beam, and she could not move. Then Gopher turned her power off completely!

EVE and WALL•E lay motionless. Gopher activated his suspension beam and lifted the two into the air. Then he dumped them both down the trash chute.

"You are confined to quarters, Captain," Auto said, locking the Captain below as he took control of the bridge.

The situation was not just bad. It was really, horribly bad.

CHAPTER 13

WALL•E woke up slowly, his systems struggling to recover. Where was he?

He heard deep, distant mechanical sounds. Looking around, he saw a huge dark room filled with piles of trash. This was the garbage bay. Then he noticed two gigantic trash compactors. They were WALL•As (Waste Allocation Load Lifters, *Axiom* class)—giant state-of-the-art versions of him. Each one could cube a ton of trash at a time.

Wow! WALL•E thought weakly. Despite his injuries, he stared at the WALL•As in amazement.

WALL·E wondered why he couldn't move. It wasn't just because he was hurt, he realized. He was also cubed into a massive block of trash! "WALL·E!" someone called. WALL·E looked to one side. EVE was cubed into another giant block nearby. Although she looked hurt, she was alert. Her systems had just rebooted, and she was trying her hardest to get free.

But now, both their cubes were moving, headed for the air lock. They were about to be ejected into space!

Eee-vaahh! WALL•E called silently. He wanted to help EVE, but he was too weak.

As the two cubes entered the air lock, WALL•E heard a loud *KA-BLAMM!* EVE had blasted free from her cube!

EVE flew to WALL•E and pulled him desperately. Finally, he came loose. But could they get safely back inside? The air lock's outer doors were shuddering, about to open. Soon WALL•E and EVE would be sucked into space and lost forever!

That was when M-O arrived. WALL•E could see the little robot racing through the garbage bay. Even as WALL•E was about to get shot into oblivion, M-O was still desperate to clean him.

Could things get any worse?

CHAPTER 14

M-O rushed straight toward WALL•E in the air lock. The air lock's inner doors were almost closed. M-O leaned forward, racing to reach WALL•E in time.

Then the inner doors stopped closing. M-O's cleaning brush was wedged tightly between the doors, holding them open!

Still clinging to WALL•E with one hand, EVE lunged to grab M-O's cleaning brush with the other. Behind them, the outer air-lock doors opened, and the gigantic trash cubes rocketed into space.

While M-O wedged the air lock's inner

doors ever so slightly open, all three robots managed to get back inside the garbage bay.

But WALL•E was badly hurt.

EVE laid him down and carefully opened his chest panel. All his circuitry was burned, thanks to Auto. EVE could see that WALL•E needed replacement parts badly. But where could she find them? Quickly, she rose into the air and flew over the garbage bay, scanning the piles of trash for a usable circuit board.

While EVE hunted for parts, the big WALL•As focused beams of light on WALL•E so he wouldn't get lost in the trash . . . or worse, get cubed all over again. Then M-O crept up and started to clean WALL•E very gently. He was trying to be a friend, not just a cleaning machine. Somehow, WALL•E had inspired even M-O to see the world differently.

At last, EVE returned, carrying an armful of circuit boards. But before she got to work, she extended her hand. She understood what

WALL•E had wanted. Now she wanted to hold hands, too.

But instead of offering his hand in return, WALL•E opened his chest—and revealed the plant! He had kept it safe all this time. Even weak and injured, he still wanted EVE to complete her directive.

But EVE no longer cared about her directive. She cared about WALL•E. Her new mission was to save *him*. Tossing the plant aside, she began trying to repair him.

"Rrrrr . . ." WALL•E tried to speak. "Rrrrrrrr . . ."

EVE listened carefully and at last understood what WALL•E was trying to say: "Earth!" If she really wanted to repair WALL•E, she had to take him home, to Earth. That was where he kept his spare parts.

EVE grabbed the plant. She didn't need it for her directive anymore, but she did need it to help WALL•E.

Then she scooped WALL•E up in her left arm and blasted a hole in the ceiling with her right arm. M-O leaped to latch on to WALL•E, and EVE rocketed all three of them out of the garbage bay.

CHAPTER 15

The threesome flew out of the trash chute into the *Axiom*'s main corridor. As they raced along, alarms sounded. Up on the bridge, Auto watched it all on his holo-screen.

"Not possible," he said.

Trapped in his quarters, the Captain saw the commotion on his holo-screen as well. "The plant!" He gasped with joy.

WALL•E, EVE, and M-O sped through the ship's halls. But the steward-bots were close behind! Luckily, WALL•E's music recorder started playing, inspiring all the reject-bots to come out of hiding. Using all their strengths (and their quirks), the reject-bots battled the stewards, allowing EVE and WALL•E to escape.

That was when the Captain took action. He lured Auto downstairs. Then he tackled Auto and held on to him with all his feeble might. After a wild struggle, both the Captain and Auto ended up on the bridge.

Auto pressed a button on the control panel. On the lower decks, even more stewards emerged. WALL•E, EVE, and the reject-bots were caught in the stewards' freeze beams.

But the Captain wouldn't give up! Even as he fought Auto, he stretched toward the control panel and pushed . . . the holo-detector button!

Instantly, the holo-detector began to rise from the lido deck. The passengers' hover chairs started following illuminated routes toward the deck. The chairs would not stop, even when they knocked over the steward-bots. As the steward-bots fell, their freeze beams dissolved. EVE and WALL•E were free!

When the passengers arrived on the lido deck, they could see their captain on a huge holo-graphic screen.

"Ladies and gentlemen, this is your captain speaking," the Captain said as he rode the bucking and kicking autopilot. "Remain seated. Just . . . a slight . . . delay! Stand by!"

But Auto fought hard. He spun around very fast, flinging the Captain into a corner . . . and tipping the entire ship! Passengers fell out of their chairs. Even EVE fell backward, the plant sliding away from her. WALL•E clung desperately to the holo-detector.

Auto moved to the control panel and hit the holo-detector button again. Now it began to move back down! But just as it was closing, WALL•E crawled beneath it, using all his strength. He knew the machine needed to stay up so that EVE could drop the plant into it.

Still, how long could WALL•E hold up the holo-detector?

Suddenly, the Captain struggled . . . rose to his feet . . . and actually walked, slowly and shakily, toward Auto. The passengers cheered.

Unsteadily, the Captain finally reached Auto and grabbed him. A small panel fell open, just above Auto's wheel. It was the master switch. The Captain knew exactly what to do: He switched Auto off! At last, the Captain was at the helm of the *Axiom* all by himself. Down on the lido deck, as the ship tipped back to an even keel, the crowd cheered again.

But where was the plant? Finally, M-O found it, and then everyone worked together to pass it to EVE. She raced to the holo-detector and—at last—placed the plant inside.

"Plant origin verified," the ship's computer announced. "Set course for Earth."

The Captain set the ship for top speed, heading for Earth. The *Axiom* was going home!

But not all was well: WALL·E had been crushed by the holo-detector.

CHAPTER 16

EVE pulled WALL•E out from under the holo-detector.

"WALL•E!" she cried. But there was no reply. As she watched, the little robot's power light faded out. WALL•E lay motionless.

As soon as the *Axiom* arrived on Earth, the Captain opened the door and showed the passengers how to walk down the ramp onto land. But EVE, M-O, and the reject-bots rushed through the crowd, heading straight toward WALL•E's truck. EVE carried WALL•E. The little robot's pet cockroach, still patiently sitting in the same spot, leaped onto his master.

Inside WALL•E's trailer, EVE gathered spare parts and began to repair him. But would it work? There was only one way to find out—she switched him on. WALL•E woke up!

"WALL•E!" EVE shouted with glee.

But WALL•E stared at her blankly.

"Eee-vah," she cried, pointing to herself. Still WALL•E didn't seem to recognize her. Could he have forgotten her? EVE handed WALL•E the lightbulb from his collection. He just looked at it.

EVE knew one thing he would remember. Quickly, she found WALL•E's videotape of *Hello, Dolly!* and popped it into the VCR. Music filled the truck as EVE eagerly turned back to her friend.

But WALL•E wasn't paying attention to the music. Instead, he was compacting all the treasures he'd spent years collecting. He squeezed, and out popped a cube of crushed items, including the lightbulb. Then he turned and motored down the truck's ramp . . . right over his pet cockroach! The little bug popped up, fine again almost immediately, but WALL•E didn't even look back.

WALL•E was alive, but something was terribly wrong. This was not the helpful, caring WALL•E that EVE knew. Had his memory been destroyed? Was he too badly damaged?

EVE followed WALL•E outside and tried one last time to get his attention. But it was no use. EVE couldn't believe that after everything they had been through together, the WALL•E she had grown to love was gone forever. Sadly, she took WALL•E's hand in hers. She leaned forward, and her head gently touched his. A little spark passed between them.

EVE pulled back. But WALL•E's fingers, still touching her hand, moved slightly. And then they moved again. "Eee . . . vah?" WALL•E asked slowly, as if waking up after a long sleep.

EVE was overjoyed. WALL•E was back!

Behind them, the gang of reject-bots approached. Then they saw EVE and WALL•E leaning their heads together tenderly, and hastily, they backed away.

Back at the *Axiom,* the Captain was having trouble coaxing the passengers out of the ship. But the children were excited and ran out first. The Captain happily started telling them about farming. With a little luck and a little hard work, the land would soon be covered with all kinds of vegetation.

WALL•E and EVE sat atop the trailer and watched the sunset, holding hands. Both had accomplished their directives . . . though WALL•E still had more cleanup work to do. Most important, they were together. And they had their new friends, the reject-bots, too.

Plants were sprouting. People were walking, ready to farm and build. Robots were ready to help clean up. Soon Earth would bloom again. And it was all because of one little robot with a great big heart.